The Frog Prince

Retold by
Susanna Davidson

Illustrated by
Mike Gordon

Reading Consultant: Alison Kelly
Roehampton University

Contents

Chapter 1

Princess in trouble

Princess Poppy was furious. "I won't marry him, Daddy," she said. "He's smelly and smug and slimier than a frog."

"You don't have to marry Prince Humperdink now, darling," said her mother. "You can wait until you're grown up."

"I *never* want to marry him," said Poppy. "I'd rather eat my toenails."

"Poppy!" shouted her father. "Don't be so rude! You've been pampered by your mother, spoiled by your sisters..."

It's time you did as I say.

"Don't be mean to Poppy, Papa," cried her sisters.

"And Humperdink has such big teeth," wailed Poppy.

"It's because I'm the youngest," Poppy went on, sadly. "My sisters got all the best princes."

"That's enough!" said the King. "Prince Humperdink is coming to dinner tonight and you *must* be polite to him. He is your future husband, after all."

"I'll find another prince to marry!" Poppy declared.

"You can have until tomorrow morning," said the King. "But you'll never find a prince in that time."

"Just you wait," said Poppy. She picked up her golden ball and stomped into the garden.

Chapter 2

Poppy's promise

Princess Poppy ran down
the path to the palace pond,
throwing and catching her
ball as she went.

"There must be another prince somewhere," she thought.

Anyone would be better than Humperdink!

Poppy was so cross, she didn't see the wobbly stone.

She wibbled...

...she wobbled.

She slipped and fell...

S P L A T

...face-first into the pond.

Her beautiful golden ball flew out of her hands. With a loud splash, it disappeared into the deep, dark pond.

I hope it doesn't land on me.

"Oh no!" Poppy groaned. "My birthday present from Daddy."

"I'm in big trouble now," she thought. Poppy looked down into the pond, hoping to see her ball.

Instead, she came face to face with a pair of big, bulging eyes.

"Urgh!" she cried. "A frog."

The frog cleared his throat.
"Princess Poppy," he croaked.
"Let me help you."

Poppy stared in surprise.
"I've never met a talking frog
before," she said. "Still... I don't
see how you could help me."

"I can fetch your ball for you," said the frog.

"Oh," said Poppy. "Thank you."

I suppose you might be useful after all.

"But you must promise me something first," he added.

"Anything, anything!" agreed Poppy.

"Promise that you'll let me live in your palace. I want to eat from your plate, drink from your glass and sleep on your silken pillow."

Yuck.

"In your dreams," thought Poppy. But out loud she said, "I promise."

Chapter 3

Frog to the rescue

The frog pushed down on his feet, leaped up with his legs and plunged into the pond.

Princess Poppy waited.
Suddenly in the deep, blue
water, she saw a glimmer
of gold.

Ta da!

The frog
rose out of the
pond. Above his
head, he held the golden ball.

"Hooray!" shouted Poppy.
She snatched up the ball and
raced back to the palace.

"Hey!" the frog called
after her. "What about
your promise?"

19

But Poppy was already too
far away to hear. The frog
hopped as fast as he could,
but he couldn't catch up
with Poppy.

Chapter 4

Into the palace

Poppy arrived back just in
time to change for dinner.

She had to sit next to Prince Humperdink, who smelled of cabbage.

Greetings, Princess Poppy.

Just then, there was a faint tapping sound.

"Is someone at the door?" asked the Queen.

22

Poppy had a sinking feeling.
She rushed to the door, opened
it and peered outside.

"Hello," said the frog.
Poppy slammed the door
in his face.

"Who was that?" said the King.
"No one," Poppy said quickly.
"That's funny," said Prince
Humperdink. "I was sure I
heard someone."

Sshh!

The tapping noise came again.
"Poppy, I really do think
someone's there," said the Queen.

24

"I'll ask the footman to look," said the King.

"No, Daddy don't!" cried Poppy. "It's only a frog."

"He rescued my golden ball from the pond," Poppy added, "and... I... sort of said he could stay with me."

25

"Then you must keep your word," bellowed the King. "Let the frog in."

I'd really rather you didn't.

"Oh Daddy, I can't," said Poppy. "He's so wet and warty..."

"Poppy!" said her father, furiously. "Let that frog in right now."

Poppy dragged her feet to
the door, praying that the frog
had gone.

But as soon as she opened
the door, the frog shot inside.

He followed Poppy all the way back to her chair. She could hear his wet feet going splat, splat, splat, on the floor behind her.

"Oh dear!" said Prince Humperdink. "Suddenly, I'm not very hungry."

I think I might be allergic to frogs.

"Excuse me," said the frog, "but Princess Poppy did promise that I could eat from her plate. May I sit at the table too?"

"Certainly not," snapped Poppy, crossly.

"Don't be so rude," said the King.

The frog is our guest.

"I'm starving," said the frog.
"What's the first course?"

"Cold watercress soup," said
the King, smiling at him.
"Help yourself!"

This is the life!

The frog dived into Poppy's
bowl. "This is delicious!" he
cried, between mouthfuls.

"I don't think I'm hungry anymore," said Poppy, as the frog slurped up the last of her soup.

I think I'm going to be sick.

"Right," said the frog cheerfully. "What's next?"
Poppy sighed miserably. "What is the second course?" she asked a maid.

32

"Um... er," the maid began
nervously.

"Come on!" said the King.
"You must know what's
for supper."

"Well you see, your
highness," the maid went on,
"Cook didn't know about our
extra guest... I'm afraid... it's
frogs' legs."

The frog gulped. "I think I might skip this course," he said, weakly.

Poppy didn't usually like frogs' legs, but that night she had seconds.

You must be full now.

"Isn't it time for bed, Princess?" said the frog.

"Oh no!" cried Poppy. "You're not coming anywhere near my bedroom."

"But you promised..." said the frog.

You can carry me on a cushion.

Poppy looked at her father pleadingly.

"Come on, dear," said the Queen. "Don't make Poppy touch that green, slimy..."

"Princesses don't break promises," interrupted the King, sternly.

Poppy took a deep breath. Then stretching out her arm, she picked up the frog by one foot.

Her sisters gasped.

"She touched him!" moaned Prince Humperdink, and fainted.

Chapter 5

The frog prince

Poppy dropped the frog in the darkest, most distant corner of her room, before climbing into bed.

"But Princess Poppy," said
the frog. "You promised I could
sleep on your silken pillow."
Poppy didn't answer.

"If you don't
let me," the
frog threatened,
"I'll tell your
father."

"I've had enough!"
snapped Poppy.
"You're the meanest,
ugliest, most horrible
frog I've ever met."

"What's more," she added, "if you mention my promise one more time, I'll throw you out of the window."

"No you won't," said the frog. "You wouldn't dare."

Your promise!

"I do dare," said Poppy. In a fury, she strode over to the frog, picked him up and threw him out of her window.

There was a long
silence, followed by
a loud splat. Poppy
suddenly realized
what she'd done.
She was horrified.

Frog? Say
something!

"I hope I haven't killed
him," she prayed, and raced
down the stairs as fast as her
legs could carry her.

40

Outside, the frog was lying
sprawled on the palace lawn.
Poppy picked him up, as
gently as she could.

"Are you all right?" she
whispered.

"Yes," croaked the frog, carefully feeling his head.

"I didn't mean to hurt you," said Poppy. "I'm so sorry." And she bent down and kissed him.

There was a loud crash of thunder, followed by a shower of sparks. The frog had vanished. In his place stood a handsome young prince.

42

"At last!" shouted the Prince. "I'm human again. No more slimy skin, no more webbed feet, no more flies..."

One by one, the palace windows flew open and everyone looked out.

"What's going on?" yelled the King. "I'm coming down."

"What happened to you?" Poppy asked the Prince.

"A wicked witch cast an evil spell on me," he said. "I could only become human again if a princess kissed me."

"So it's because of me that you're a prince again?" said Poppy, feeling rather proud.

"Well, yes," said the Prince, "but you did throw me out of the window first."

"Still," said Poppy, "there aren't many princesses who would kiss a frog."

"Excuse me," said Prince
Humperdink, "but Poppy is
going to marry ME."

"No I'm not," said Poppy.
"It hasn't been arranged yet.
And Daddy, you did say I
could find my own prince."

"That's true," said the King,
with a sigh.

"In that case," said the
Prince, getting down on one
knee. "If you promise not to
throw me out of the window
again..."

I promise.

"...Princess Poppy, will
you marry me?"

"I will," said Poppy.
And she did.

The tale of *The Frog Prince* has been around since the thirteenth century. It was told by storytellers all over Europe. This version is from the retelling by Jacob and Wilhelm Grimm, two brothers who lived in Germany in the early 1800s.

Series editor: Lesley Sims

Designed by Katarina Dragoslavic

Cover design by Russell Punter

First published in 2005 by Usborne Publishing Ltd., Usborne House, 83-85 Saffron Hill, London EC1N 8RT, England. www.usborne.com
Copyright © 2005 Usborne Publishing Ltd.

48